Parent's Introduction

Whether your child is a beginning reader, a reluctant reader, or an eager reader, this book offers a fun and easy way to encourage and help your child in reading.

Developed with reading education specialists, *We Both Read* books invite you and your child to take turns reading aloud. You read the left-hand pages of the book, and your child reads the right-hand pages—which have been written at one of six early reading levels. The result is a wonderful new reading experience and faster reading development!

You may find it helpful to read the entire book aloud yourself the first time, then invite your child to participate the second time. As you read, try to make the story come alive by reading with expression. This will help to model good fluency. It will also be helpful to stop at various points to discuss what you are reading. This will help increase your child's understanding of what is being read.

In some books, a few challenging words are introduced in the parent's text, distinguished with **bold** lettering. Pointing out and discussing these words can help to build your child's reading vocabulary. If your child is a beginning reader, it may be helpful to run a finger under the text as each of you reads. Please also notice that a "talking parent" 👪 icon precedes the parent's text, and a "talking child" 👶 icon precedes the child's text.

If your child struggles with a word, you can encourage "sounding it out," but keep in mind that not all words can be sounded out. Your child might pick up clues about a word from the picture, other words in the sentence, or any rhyming patterns. If your child struggles with a word for more than five seconds, it is usually best to simply say the word.

Most of all, remember to praise your child's efforts and keep the reading fun. After you have finished the book, ask a few questions and discuss what you have read together. Rereading this book multiple times may also be helpful for your child.

Try to keep the tips above in mind as you read together, but don't worry about doing everything right. Simply sharing the enjoyment of reading together will increase your child's reading skills and help to start your child off on a lifetime of reading enjoyment!

The Well-Mannered Monster

A We Both Read Book
Level 1
Guided Reading: Level E

To our parents, who read us our first books.

Text Copyright © 2006 by Marcy Brown and Dennis Haley
Illustrations Copyright © 2006 by Tim Raglin
All rights reserved

We Both Read® is a trademark of Treasure Bay, Inc.

Published by Treasure Bay, Inc.
P.O. Box 119
Novato, CA 94948 USA

Printed in Malaysia

Library of Congress Catalog Card Number: 2005905160

ISBN: 978-1-891327-66-7

Visit us online at WeBothRead.com

PR-10-18

WE BOTH READ®

The Well-Mannered Monster

By Marcy Brown and Dennis Haley

Illustrated by Tim Raglin

TREASURE BAY

My name is Pat and this is Matt. He is my very best friend in the whole world. He also just happens to be a **monster.**

He is a big **monster** and he is a fun **monster**.

I like being best friends with Matt. Even though he is a monster, he has very good **manners.** When we play with our friends, Matt makes sure everyone gets a chance to play.

He takes turns. Taking turns is good **manners.**

Matt always plays fair and never breaks the rules. Sometimes he wins. Sometimes he doesn't. If he doesn't win, he is still happy to have played and is never a poor sport.

That is why it is fun to play with Matt.

One day my mother was making a very special dinner. There were pots and pans and plates everywhere. She was working very hard, so Matt **asked** if we **could** help.

Mom said, "Yes." She **asked** if we **could** go to the store for her.

Mom gave us a list of what she needed. She reminded us that it was a long way to the store. We were going to have to cross the street. Matt said we **would** be very careful.

Matt said he **would** hold my hand. He always does when we cross the street.

On the way we saw my mailman, Mr. Bell. I said "Hello," and Matt said, "Hello," too. He waved as big as he could, but Mr. Bell did not wave back.

Mr. Bell did not know Matt. He had never met a monster.

Matt knew the polite thing to do was to introduce himself. He told Mr. Bell that his name was Matt and that it was nice to **meet** him. Then he shook his hand.

Mr. Bell was happy to **meet** Matt. He was glad to know his name.

After we saw Mr. Bell, we saw a lady standing outside of the store. She was carrying such a big box that she could not **open** the door by herself. Matt knew just what to do.

He **opened** the door for her. "**After** you," he said.

In the store was a man who wanted a box of soap. It was way up high on the top shelf. He tried to reach it, but he couldn't.

So Matt and I helped him.
It is good to help if you can.
You can help if you are big
or small.

After we were done shopping, we met the store owner. He said he had been worried about having a monster in his store, but he was not worried anymore.

He said that Matt was a very nice monster. He was happy to have Matt shop at his store.

On our way home, we saw our friend, Rose. She wanted us to play ball. We thanked her, but said we had **promised** to go straight home.

We gave our word to Mom.
We were going to keep our
promise.

Dinner was ready. Matt and I helped to bring out the food. By the time we were finished, there was so much food it covered the whole table.

It was a lot of food,
even for a monster!

The doorbell rang and Matt answered it. There were lots of **people** at the door! There were our neighbors and our mailman, Mr. Bell. Mom had invited all of them over for dinner.

We had lots of food. We had lots of **people**. Now we could have dinner!

I helped people with their chairs. Mom gave everyone fresh ice water. Matt put his napkin on his lap and didn't take a bite until everyone had their food.

Manners are nice. They show people that you care.

Sometimes, even after everyone has their food, they need one more thing. Matt needed **butter** for his bread. He knew he could reach across the table for it, but he decided to say **"please"** instead.

He asked Mr. Bell to **please** pass the **butter**. Then he said, "Thank you."

Mr. Bell said, "You are welcome."

When anyone spoke to Matt, he listened with both of his ears. He waited until they were done **talking** before he spoke. He did not ever interrupt.

All of us like to **talk**.
It is good to take turns.

Finally my mom brought out dessert. She had used the sugar we bought to make chocolate chip **cookies**! She'd made a special one for Matt!

Matt said, "Thank you."
He likes **cookies**. He likes
big **cookies** even more.

Even if your food tastes great, no one wants to see it in your mouth. I always try to keep my **mouth** closed while I am eating.

Matt does too. He does not talk with his **mouth** full and he uses his napkin.

All the guests thanked my mom, Matt and me for a wonderful dinner. We said, "You're welcome." Then Matt and I thanked my mother in our own way, by **helping** to wash the dishes.

Helping is another way to say, "Thank you." It can be fun too!

Before we went to sleep, Matt wrote a thank-you note to my mother for his special cookie. Then he thanked me for making him a part of such a wonderful day. He really is a nice and well-mannered monster.

That is why I like him.

If you liked *The Well-Mannered Monster,* here are some other We Both Read books you are sure to enjoy!

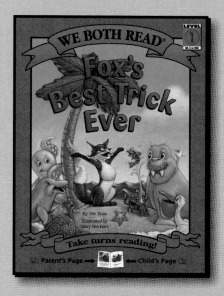

To see all the We Both Read books that are available,
just go online to **www.WeBothRead.com**.